ABOUT ALICE

by Charles Laurence

A SAMUEL FRENCH ACTING EDITION

SAMUEL FRENCH

FOUNDED 1830

New York Hollywood London Toronto

SAMUELFRENCH.COM

ISBN   978-0-573-62632-6   Printed   in   U.S.A.   #3848

MUSIC USE NOTE

IMPORTANT BILLING AND CREDIT REQUIREMENTS

CHARACTERS

ALICE HOGAN
48. an ex-artist's model still retaining a lot of her beauty. Impulsive, funny and honest. Now adrift and unsettled after the death of the love of her life.

NED JONES
60. Thin and wiry. Neat dresser, sharp tongued, a little pedantic. Intelligent, civilized, casts a jaundiced eye over life.

PEGGY BLACK
31. A business woman. Plain hard-shell exterior, emotionally confused interior. Bright, Swiss-American education. Tries hard to appear efficient and in control.

JOSEPH PANAMA
31. A man not a boy. Good body, great charm and sex appeal. Open, uncomplicated, happy very much at ease with his lifesty.le. His date of birth in Act II Sc. 2 should be adjusted to keep him 31 years old.

SETTING

ACT I
Scene.1. Alice Hogan's Living Room.
Early Afternoon of the 14th of July
Scene 2. The same. Early Evening

ACT II
Scene 1. Alice Hogan's Living Room. The Next Morning
Scene 2. The same. Three hours later

ACT I

Scene 1

(ALICE HOGAN's living room. In a Victorian house behind
Sloane Square. Center right back, door leading from hall.
Stage left, back shelved wall unit with bottles of drink, books
and a scuptured head. Whole back wall covered with framed
paintings and drawings. Aslant to corner stage left, glass
doors leading to paved area of garden, tub of shrubs, part
of a yellow brick wall. Stage left, a Victorian tiled fireplace,
crammed with photos, notes, postcards.
In front of patio doors, a battered, squashed chesterfield with
Oriental cushions, narrow long table behind. In front a low
round painted table. Center right, a bentwood Thonet chair.
Stage right, a day bed and a small desk. Stripped floor-
boards and Turkey rugs. An 'artistic' room developed over
many years. An Eileen Gray lamp, maquettes, the odd
Augustus John drawing and Paul Nash watercolor.)

(ALICE HOGAN, 48, dressed mainly in black with a hat enters hurriedly and with purpose. Telephone is ringing, she
ignores it, moves straight to drinks. Takes glass from unit,
pours a neat vodka, has a swig and moves to look out over

garden. She stands still and silent.)

*(NED JONES enters, 60, grey suit, black tie. Thin and wiry.
He stays by the door, looks at ALICE's back then at the
ringing phone.)*

NED. Do you want me to answer it?
ALICE. No.

*(She wheels round, presses phone and it stops. A distant ring-
ing continues. ALICE resumes her hugging pose by the
garden.)*

NED. It's still ringing in the kitchen.
ALICE. Let the cat deal with it.
NED. How can you ignore it? It might be important.
ALICE. I used to spend half my life being dragged out of
the shower for trivia. No more.
NED. I can't bear it. I'll say you're out and take a message.
(Phone stops ringing as he reaches it.) It's stopped. I do so
hate it when it does that.
ALICE. Drown your sorrows.
NED. I don't usually drink before lunch.
ALICE. You are idiotic at times. *(She turns back to stare at
the garden. He stares at the phone. Suddenly she grabs the
hat off her head and flings it violently away across the room.)*
Why did I wear a bleeding hat? Nobody else did.
NED. We belong to the old school, my dear Alice. Besides,
you were the only woman present.
ALICE. No, I wasn't.
NED. Virtually, if one omits the corpse and the dwarfish

distant cousin who inherits everything.

ALICE. Don't grudge her some good fortune—dreary, short arsed creature. She didn't have a hat.

NED. She wore a dangerously ill-fitting wig, that's a covering of sorts.

ALICE. Gloria's legs were so long.

NED. And so busy.

ALICE. True. While we were waiting for the coffin to do it's disappearing act, I had a good look round—I swear everyone there was an ex-lover. That would have pleased her.

NED. An orgy of mourners. What about the lad, Geoffrey?

ALICE. Mmmm. Half term at Harrow. Gloria drove down in a dormobile and took his cherry in a lay-by. The darling. God, I'll miss her.

NED. I was there.

ALICE. At Harrow?

NED. At the crematorium.

ALICE. I know. We went together, remember?

NED. And my presence there was that of an old friend not a dubious conquest.

ALICE. Yes I see but we all know about your problem. Are you going to stare at that perishing phone all day?

NED. I'm waiting for them to ring back.

ALICE. Why should they?

NED. Because I always do. In case it was a wrong number the first time.

ALICE. You are strange... I'd forgotten.

NED. We only meet at funerals nowadays.

(ALICE sits on sofa and tucks her legs up under.)

ALICE. Well, I suppose poor Gloria's flying up the crematorium chimney by now.

NED. Why is it that whenever I see a coffin perched in a chapel of rest, I half expect a magician to appear and saw it in half?

ALICE. That isn't nice. I wouldn't mind a few conjuring tricks though to liven things up, funerals are so damned gloomy.

NED. One school of thought has it that they're extremely randy making.

ALICE. My loins remained unstirred throughout. What about yours? Sorry, I forgot, that's an unfair question.

NED. It's a simple theory that the Grim Reaper Death is a vivid reminder of our own mortality and it triggers off a basic need to procreate thus ensuring the survival of the species.

ALICE. Really? The gathering we attended afterwards wasn't exactly wild, was it?

NED. We did leave early.

ALICE. And then they all shouted, 'Thank God those two dreary buggers have gone', and leapt upon each other? I refuse to believe it.

NED. Most things are possible. As you should know.

ALICE. If it were true, undertakers and their staff would be at it like knives all the time.

NED. Who's to say they aren't? I doubt very much if anyone's conducted an opinion poll on the degrees of sexual satisfaction among morticians wives.

ALICE. I shall have a jolly good look the next funeral I go to, unless it's my own of course.

NED. Much more likely to be mine.

ALICE. Don't be selfish. I need you on this earth to hold my hand if and when I decide to take the jelly babies.

NED. Jelly babies?
ALICE. Prettily colored barbiturates to you.

(She holds up her glass.)

NED. Do you want topping up?
ALICE. Nothing to top.

(NED takes her glass and pours drink. He pours himself a large brandy.)

NED. I'm going to allow myself a medicinal Armagnac.
ALICE. Good.
NED. Nothing with your vodka?
ALICE. I need the undiluted fire. *(He hands her drink.)* Thanks.
NED. Are you serious about swallowing a handful of sleeping pills?
ALICE. Oh Ned, you shouldn't have gone to live in France, we have lost touch. I keep a small case handy like an expectant mother. Clean nightie stroke shroud, hairbrush, photo of Hogan, bottle of vodka and a modest but sufficient supply of death sweeties. Shocked?
NED. Puzzled. Why?
ALICE. Dunno. In case the mirage fails me and I see the true desert of my life.
NED. Suicide is giving up.
ALICE. What's wrong with that? Not British? Animals give up all the time in the face of overwhelming odds.
NED. Personally, I prefer persistence, it is the active form of patience.

ALICE. You're the sort that crumbles on till you're only a brain in a jar. Don't expect me to visit you than.

NED. Little point, I wouldn't know where to put the grapes.

ALICE. Oh God! In future I'm only going to attend the funerals of people I hate.

NED. And smirk happily throughout?

ALICE. Yes; kick all the flowers about and dance a jig on the grave.

NED. A soft shoe shuffle on the ashes.

ALICE. Brilliant! What a jokey way to scatter them.

NED. Add a codicil to your will.

ALICE. That's all settled. Medical science get my bits and pieces.

NED. Highly altruistic.

ALICE. It's such a good bargain—no burial expenses, no floral tributes and no crocodile tears.

NED. But you're loaded with money and have no immediate family to benefit.

ALICE. True.

NED. So cough up the real reason.

ALICE. A lazy way to do some good at the end. My life so far has been singularly short on noble gestures.

NED. You put up with Hogan for over thirty years and nursed him to that bitter end. That must be worth enough brownie points to positively whizz you through the Pearly Gates.

ALICE. He needed me... a happy, happy need.

NED. I seem to recall some toughy, toughy moments.

ALICE. It was a true relationship, I was so lucky. Leaving Hogan would have been like dumping a puppy on the fast lane of a motorway—unthinkable.

NED. Edith had no such qualms, she loved him for twenty years and left him flat.

ALICE. Oh no, Edith was bright, huh, was she bright? Without my realizing it she'd trained me very thoroughly as a replacement before she bolted.

NED. You could have done the same later.

ALICE. I didn't want to. I loved him.

NED. All the more reason to resent that perpetual procession of pubescent girls.

ALICE. Ned, remember I was cabbage green, a country lass of sixteen. I thought all artists lived like that. And he gave me total freedom in return, the very idea of jealously made him laugh.

NED. Still, that endless supply of firm flesh, like an early experiment in factory farming.

ALICE. I positively enjoyed the pimping and procuring. I was good at it, much better than Edith with her New England puritanism.

NED. I'm amazed you could sleep nights.

ALICE. Why?

NED. Guilt my dear Alice, guilt. Those girls weren't tarts.

ALICE. They weren't coerced or drugged either and all were of legal age or thereabouts. Hogan was a wonderful experience for a young girl, kind, gentle and marvelously masculine in bed, never a worry about what to do next, he either did it or told you to do it.

NED. Like I said, lambs to the slaughter.

ALICE You're a moral vegetarian. Most women lose their virginity in a state of embarrassed politeness tinged with anxiety. They simply don't have the vocabulary to resist. As long as the man makes no crude or sudden moves, the majority of well brought up young maidens think it rude to interrupt a seduction. Halfway through remarking upon the mildness of the weather they find their knickers round their ankles.

NED. Unbelievable.

ALICE. Even though you don't indulge, you can surely appreciate the theory of sex?

NED. So?

ALICE. So why the wild cry of unbelievable as if I'd just performed a Catholic Contraception Dance?

NED. Sorry, my mind had wandered. I was thinking back to Edith Hogan and the sinister way in which she disappeared... vanished completely... overnight... without a trace.

ALICE. Foul play was not suspected, Ned.

NED. Maybe. I do know my mind raced like a mill stream. *(He moves to windows.)* How pretty the garden looks. You were clever to have all that York stone laid down so soon after Edith... departed.

ALICE. *(Laughing.)* You are a pig. You know very well Hogan got the final divorce papers from her a year later. Reno—Nevada, you thought it common.

NED. But never a single word of explanation. Mysteries offend me.

ALICE. For heaven's sake it's thirty odd years ago. Edith got lost in the melting pot of them old United States. Maybe she got homesick, who knows?

NED. Homesick for America? There's not a jury in the land would swallow that.

ALICE. You've never been there, you fraud.

NED. I've seen the moving pictures. Homesick indeed! Just possible I suppose, twenty years of marriage to macho Man Hogan would be enough to turn any woman's mind.

ALICE. Don't be vile. She endured the hard years in Paris and Prague. I had the rich, cushy time in London.

NED. Quite right, you were after all responsible for his greatest successes. You and your celebrated knee-length hair.

ALICE. I was only the model, he was the genius.

NED. Ha! There's nothing like death for bumping up a reputation—temporarily.

ALICE. You still delight in being perverse. Shut up and pour me a drink, Ned.

(NED takes the glasses and fills them.)

NED. You do realize we're going to end up drunk?

ALICE. Do you have a better idea? This is a wake.

NED. Cheers. Where is your hair by the way? At my last visit it was pinned rather ostentatiously across most of that wall.

ALICE. I took it down and put it away in a drawer. It was a dreadful dust trap.

NED. How wise. I thought it looked like something you'd shot.

ALICE. Philistine! My hair is a piece of Art History, I could sell it at Southeby's. There are five paintings and three sculptures of it in the Tate alone and by four different artists.

NED. Follicle fetishists to a man.

ALICE. *(Laughs.)* I like 'follicle fetishist'', even if it is a bugger to say. You do sing for your supper nicely, Ned. How long are you planning on staying?

NED. Is a week alright?

ALICE. That'll fly by. Is it your mad theory then that Hogan was kinky for hair?

NED. You tell me. It was most definitely the gimmick he worked to death in his later and commercially successful work.

ALICE. A great sculptor doesn't need gimmicks.

NED. I rest my case.

ALICE. The world disagrees with you, so change the subject.

NED. You're looking good. I did so hate that ridiculous hair hanging down your bum reminiscent of some endangered species of water mammal.

ALICE. Please, I was considered a famous beauty.

NED. Did it itch a lot in bed?

ALICE. It kept an army of lovers warm.

NED. I would have suspected that it got painfully in the way like sand.

ALICE. Ned, I know it was about thirty years ago and we didn't make a habit of it—but can't you remember?

NED. I can recollect the fact but little about the act.

ALICE. I keep a vivid memory of the aftermath.

NED. It was always so with me. Did it hurt you to cut it off? Emotionally.

ALICE. I felt nothing but the breeze on my neck. A semi-symbolic act after Hogan died.

NED. Eight years ago yesterday, do you realize?

ALICE. No need to remind *me*, it did happen to be the day before my birthday.

NED. Oh... then Many Happy Returns of Today.

ALICE. Thanks. Huh, Happy Returns, Happy Christmas, Happy New Year... what's so bloody special about happiness that they keep shoving it down our throats?

NED. Another capitalist plot, I dare say—fellatio for the masses.

I usually cry on my birthday.

NED. If you're determined to be morbid, just one or two Happy Returns Alice. Is that better?

ALICE. I was born under an ill fated star, disaster always strikes around this time.

NED. Superstitious nonsense.

ALICE. Oh yes? Sheer coincidence I suppose that my mother died dishing out the trifle at my 13th birthday party?

NED. You're making that up. She didn't, did she?

ALICE. She did. I've also slipped a disc, been mugged, had a miscarriage, broken a wrist, lost Hogan, put down two dear cats and now buried my best friend Gloria, all on or around the date of my birth. What do you say to that?

NED. You make it sound as if it all occurred on one dreadfully busy day.

ALICE. That really would be sanatorium time. Lolling quietly in the corner wheelchair dribbling into my patchwork.

NED. Don't dwell on it. Be like me, I seldom remember dates.

ALICE. One hardly needs to be a bloody elephant to remember the 14th of July.

NED. The day they stormed the Bastille!

ALICE. Precisely. The French have always been ghastly, how can you live there?

NED. I like my food.

ALICE. Is that a hint?

NED. Heavens, no. The sausage roll I risked at the funeral feast has lodged. I'm happy with the brandy.

ALICE. What a sweet, undemanding houseguest you are.

NED. Old friends don't impose.

ALICE. They bring back memories. Do you remember

when Gloria was known as the Chelsea Bike because anyone could get a ride on her?

NED. I was under the impression the pair of you were a tandem.

ALICE. I was never that outrageous. Never. Was I?

NED. You did seem to change your lovers with the same degree of regularity as you did your bed linen.

ALICE. There was safety in numbers.

NED. No permanent involvements.

ALICE. Exactly. Hogan was the only man I ever loved or wanted to, you know that.

NED. More's the pity. *(He has refilled their glasses.)* It was rash of us to continue drinking. I shall feel the need for a little lie down soon.

ALICE. What a lovely idea, let's curl up together.

NED. You see, the funeral did make you randy, you are lusting after my poor collapsed body.

ALICE. Cross my heart, all I want is a quiet cuddle and a zizz.

NED. Don't bother to deny it, I can hear your ovaries clicking from here.

ALICE. Ned! As if I would want to put either of us through that experience again.

NED. I'm amazed that you still remember it considering the thousands in between.

ALICE. Darling, you made yourself unforgettable. Nobody else has ever pleasured me and immediately been violently ill. I had to nurse you for two whole days, that kind of behavior does tend to stick in the memory.

NED. You were warned.

ALICE. Yes but I didn't believe it, I still don't.

NED. Nothing's changed. My body posesses a natural allergy to intercourse, I've had to settle for celibacy or sex by proxy.

ALICE. Weird... and tragic.

NED. I've never felt particularly deprived, even as a child I played doctors and nurses by myself.

ALICE. It's a mystery. Sex has always made me feel so real, brought everything into sharp focus.

NED. Bully for you.

ALICE. I often wondered, did you never experiment with men?

NED. In my worried youth I tried the lot barring goats and goldfish and the result was depressingly similar—utter post coital prostration.

ALICE. I'm rather flattered that you bothered to try again with me.

NED. Aaah but you were so beautiful Alice... and determined as a ferret.

(ALICE laughs and moves back on sofa patting it.)

ALICE. Come over here or would a platonic hug give you heartburn?

NED. There are some things one has to risk.

(NED lies with ALICE and she snuggles up her head on his shoulder.)

ALICE. That's nice, you've grown more comfortable with age. I like a bit of padding.

NED. That's quite enough about me, how about you? Who

is likely to burst in and slay me in a fit of totally misplaced jealousy and rage?

ALICE. Only ghosts.

NED. You are far too young to embrace spiritualism, it's an elderly vice.

ALICE. It's true, there's no one in my life at the present. I'm laboring under the yoke of chastity.

NED. How long have you been laboring this time—a couple of weeks?

ALICE. Ages, I've changed. Simply ages. I couldn't draw you a naked man from memory.

NED. You could try the conventional life, settle down with an honest chap and give dinner parties.

ALICE. No, I'm grooved into the habit of short and sweet, physical relationships.

NED. That routine was imposed upon you through fear of losing Hogan. Hogan is dead.

ALICE. I know, I know that. But there are parts of me, deep, important parts that haven't yet fully realized the fact.

(Pause.)

NED. Have you tried acupuncture?

ALICE. I haven't 'tried' anything. Time is the great healer, so they keep telling me.

NED. I can't think why. Time eventually kills each and every one of us. Time is a mass murderer.

ALICE. The cure of oblivion. I don't know what to do, Ned.

NED. About what?

ALICE. Living. The living of life. All the old supports are

going, Gloria's irreplacable, my doctor's retired, the dentist is dead and my nice butcher has become a Buddhist. *(Telephone begins to ring.)* Who turned that on?

NED. I did. I refuse to submit myself to that torture again. *(He leans over back of sofa and picks up.)* Hello? Hogan residence... No, she's lying down. Can I take a message?... Ah yes, hello, this is Ned Jones... Ned, I came to the funeral with Alice. *(Hand over mouthpiece.)* It's the short-arsed cousin... I see... I see... Yes, I do see... No, of course, I'm sure Alice will be only too delighted and touched. Yes, do send them round... not at all. Good-bye.

(He replaces phone.)

ALICE. Sounds as if I'm getting a small token of remembrance.

NED. In a manner of speaking, yes. Darling, could you move, my leg's gone to sleep.

(ALICE leans forward, he extricates himself and stands up to stretch.)

ALICE. Don't keep me in suspense. Is it the Edward Burra pictures—I kept admiring them in a loud voice?

NED. No.

ALICE. It's not the collection of ghastly thirties teapots, is it?

NED. Rest assured, it isn't.

ALICE. Well?

NED. Gloria left no will.

ALICE. We know that.

NED. But a note has just been found stating that she wished to be cremated

ALICE. That's lucky, considering.

NED. She also wants her ashes to be scattered in a favorite place.

ALICE. Where's that?

NED. That's the problem. Cousin Shorty never even met her so as you were Gloria's closest and dearest she's arranging to send her over so you can do the honors.

(ALICE gets up quickly.)

ALICE. You're making this up.

NED. No, honestly, I'm not.

ALICE. Then why are you trying not to laugh, you sod.

NED. Because its' so *bizarre.*

ALICE. Truly?

NED. I swear on my mother's mausoleum.

ALICE. You idiot! I've never done it, I don't know how to scatter ashes.

NED. I'm sure it's something on can pick up quite easily, same action as feeding chickens I should imagine.

ALICE. Which I do constantly, of course. And I have no idea what her favorite place is... was.

NED. Think, surely she mentioned it in conversation.

ALICE. She was keen on the Savoy Grill but—No, it's ridiculous, I'm ringing back to say I can't do it.

(ALICE moves to phone, NED stops her.)

NED. Don't! Far better you should do it than some anonymous, distant relative.

ALICE. But I don't believe in funeral ritual and mumbo jumbo. The memory matters not the empty shell.

NED. Then it's no skin off your nose, is it?

ALICE. Answering the wretched telephone invariably leads to complications. Alright, I'll do it but only if you help me.

NED. I wouldn't miss it for the world.

ALICE. I'm so angry, why did Gloria have to top herself.

NED. The usual combination of courage and despair. *(Two long rings on the doorbell. NED moves towards door.)* I'll go.

ALICE. Leave it, it'll be someone selling something useless.

NED. It might be the ashes.

(NED exits. ALICE calls after him.)

ALICE. *(Sarcastically.)* Yes, very likely—red hot and smoking *(She crosses to desk and picks up small, framed photograph.)* Hogan... Hogan. I'm still lost without you, love.

(NED re-enters holding out a visiting card.)

NED. A Miss Black and friend from Harvest House to see you.

ALICE. Harvest House! Are they the Funeral Directors?

NED. Read. It's a quite reputable book publishing house. And she says she has an appointment.

ALICE. Oh, my God! She could be right... I do vaguely... recall... *(She flips through the desk diary.)* Yes, here it is. She's bang on time 2:30. I haven't looked at this since Gloria died.

NED. Shall I tell her to phone next week?

ALICE. No, too much guilt. She's been pestering me for weeks with transatlantic calls and I've already cancelled once. These publishers are mad keen to do a biography of Hogan.

NED. Sort of interesting.

ALICE. No, hopeless. I can never remember when anything happened or even if it did.

NED. I'll happily provide a definitive portrait with a plethora of warts.

ALICE. You will keep your mouth zipped. I might as well get it over with. Where are they?

NED. On the doorstep.

ALICE. Good. Let me nip upstairs to change out of these weeds, then show them in and offer them a drink.

(ALICE exits rapidly. NED follows. Voices in hall. NED ushers in PEGGY BLACK, 29, power dressed and carrying an attache case. JOSEPH PANAMA, 30ish, American, easy sex appeal, good physique, casual summer suit, camera slung round neck and carrying a canvas bag.)

NED. Mrs. Hogan won't keep you long. *(Moves to drinks.)* Would anyone like a drink?

PEGGY. I'd love a cup of coffee, milk no sugar.

NED. Ah. How about you?

JOE. Orange juice if you have it, please.

NED. I think I spotted a carton lurking in the fridge. Make yourselves comfortable.

(NED exits. JOE puts bag down by sofa and sits in center chair. PEGGY puts her case down on sofa table and wanders

nervously looking at objects. As soon as NED has left the
room PEGGY turns angrily on JOE.)

PEGGY. I can't believe what you just told me. I cannot believe it.

JOE. I assumed everything was fixed. And I did give you references.

PEGGY. It's very likely you've ruined this entire project, damn you!

JOE. I'm sorry but what the heck were you planning to say, 'Hi, Mrs. Hogan here's a little something I brought you over from the States'—and slap my gift wrapped dick in her hand?

PEGGY. Keep your voice down. I asked you if you were willing to fly to London to... to satisfy a lady, you said yes, quoted me an exorbitant overseas rate and were paid in advance, so what is this, some kind of rip off?

JOE. Miss Black, it's a simple, straightforward service I provide, you pay me money and I screw, I don't seduce. My prime rules are no gays, no unprotected sex and I never seduce.

PEGGY. What's the difference so long as you get paid?

JOE. There's a big moral difference. Besides, I can't handle dealing with illusions and emotions, it has to be purely physical—like a good workout at the gym.

(PEGGY reaches a sudden decision.)

PEGGY. Would a bonus of one thousand dollars overcome your scruples?

JOE. What do you take me for? Deceit is against my nature,

I couldn't live with myself. I don't seduce.

PEGGY. Okay, okay, you don't seduce but could you allow yourself to BE seduced?

(JOE rises and thinks.)

JOE. I guess so.

PEGGY. Thank God for that.

JOE. Wait. The situation's never arisen before, not in a business context. What do I have to do?

PEGGY. Be charming and look provocative and available. Think you can handle that?

JOE. On one condition, she has to make all the moves, every single one.

PEGGY. It's a deal. Though it would be nice if at some crucial point you could release yourself from your controlled paralysis.

JOE. That's a tricky one though, when exactly?

PEGGY. Won't be a problem—she's a slut.

JOE. Hush. You don't know the lady.

PEGGY. She used to pimp for Matthew Hogan, he had a passion for young girls.

JOE. Really! How young?

PEGGY. Nothing nasty... sixteen, seventeen and on the scrapheap at twenty.

JOE. Sad to limit oneself. There's something attractive about every woman's body if you concentrate. My range is legal till death.

PEGGY. But Hogan was a genius, you should have seen the retrospective exhibition at the Museum of Modern Art. Incredible!

JOE. Yea, I saw it.

PEGGY. Why?

JOE. I expect I wandered in to shelter form the rain, sure was a wet fall that year.

PEGGY. I suppose the nudes attracted you.

JOE. True. I had a big reaction—above the waist. The long hair twisting over and caressing the bodies, half concealing, half revealing. Great stuff.

PEGGY. Alice Hogan was his favorite model.

JOE. I bought a catalogue too. Think she still got all that hair?

PEGGY. I have no idea. *(Looks into garden.)* There's Hogan's studio, the finest American sculptor this century.

JOE. That wasn't so difficult, he and Epstein are virtually the only American sculptors, unless you rate Lipshitz.

PEGGY. I don't believe it, one minute the Happy Hooker, the next an Arts Major.

JOE. I have a lot of free time in my profession, I fill in with courses at Columbia.

PEGGY. Weird.

JOE. I've been thinking, maybe you haven't offered the lady enough money.

PEGGY. Matthew Hogan left her everything. She's sitting pretty on marbles and bronzes worth four to six million dollars.

JOE. Being rich doesn't stop people being greedy. I should know. Do I still get that thousand dollar bonus?

PEGGY. Only if you score.

JOE. Better keep my fingers crossed. No one's a universal sexual fantasy—not even me.

PEGGY. You'd certainly fail with me.

JOE. My heart is broken, Miss Black.

(PEGGY turns away. ALICE enters changed into summer dress.)

ALICE. Hello. Sorry to have kept you waiting but it's been a crowded day.

PEGGY. It's very good of you to see us. Peggy Black, editor with Harvest House, we've spoken on the phone. *(PEGGY stretches out a hand which ALICE shakes and looks at JOE, giving him her full attention.)* This is Joe Panama.

JOE. Joseph. Joe Panama sounds like some kind of cheap stud. Honored to meet you, ma'am.

ALICE. Oh Lord!

JOE Is anything the matter?

ALICE. Ma'am. It's an enchanting American custom but it does make me feel totally unapproachable or royal. Please call me Alice.

(ALICE puts out a hand which JOE takes.)

JOE. I'd be delighted to, Alice. I'm Joseph.

ALICE. Doesn't suit you. Panama is such a gift of a name, I wouldn't dream of using anything else.

PEGGY. Matthew Hogan was always called Hogan by his friends, wasn't he?

ALICE. Yes, the name fitted the man.

PEGGY. Names are so important. The wrong one can ruin a life.

ALICE. But it's so simple to change it. Far easier than one's character.

PEGGY. It's difficult in childhood, then it can be damaging.

ALICE. Children are naturally cruel, think of the horrid nicknames they invent. Please sit down. Have you been offered a drink?

PEGGY. Yes, the... the man who let us in is getting me some coffee.

ALICE. My God, I'd better rescue him, the kitchen's not his forte. Something stronger for you, Panama?

JOE. Plain orange juice for me, please. I'm not a drinker.

ALICE. Watch out young man, abstinence is the most limiting of virtues.

JOE. I'm not in any danger, I have other sinning ways.

ALICE. I guessed. Ned does appear to have got lost. Excuse me a minute.

(ALICE exits smiling at JOE.)

JOE. Happy so far?

PEGGY. She's looking at you like the cherry on an ice cream sundae.

JOE. It means nothing. The lady's a natural flirt, a dying breed. I like her.

PEGGY. Good. Open your legs wider and slide forward.

JOE. I'm the expert, let's be subtle please.

PEGGY. We don't have the time. Advertise. Look sexy.

JOE. I don't have to look sexy, I am sexy.

PEGGY. You're sure you now how to work that camera?

JOE. Yes stop worrying it's another of my hobbies.

(PEGGY is very on edge, circling the room looking at everything.)

PEGGY. What a mess. This room's like a time warp.

JOE. Why don't you loosen up a little?

PEGGY. I can't, this project is too important to me. I'm going to tell her it's your birthday so play along with it.

JOE. Why?

PEGGY. Because I'm paying. And it'll soften her up.

JOE. You planning on following me into the bedroom with any more last minute instructions?

PEGGY. Don't be stupid. I can't imagine any—

(Enter ALICE and NED who carries small tray with cup of coffee and glass of orange juice.)

ALICE. Here we are. Ned meet Peggy Black and Panama—Ned Jones a great friend.

NED. How do you do?

PEGGY. Hello.

JOE Glad to meet you.

(ALICE takes coffee to PEGGY.)

ALICE. Ned's buried himself in France of recent years, he came over to brighten up a funeral. Is that alright?

PEGGY. Fine, thanks.

JOE. Thanks.

NED. Did I hear your name right, Panama?

JOE. Yes, Joseph Panama.

ALICE. I told you not to gild the lily.

NED. I see, the Hogan syndrome.

(ALICE has freshened her drink.)

ALICE. Panama doesn't drink but he promises other vices. Please, let's all sit down.

NED. I gather you're in publishing, Mr. Panama.

JOE. No, I'm not intellectual.

NED. That's an advantage surely?

JOE. I do some work as a freelance photographer.

ALICE. That is the wickedest vice. Photographs destroy hope and illusion. I prefer memory. Romantic, kind, mercifully blurred memory.

JOE. So I don't get to take your picture?

ALICE. Your timing's way out, unfortunately. By about twenty years.

JOE. There's no reason to do it but I could smear the lens with vaseline.

ALICE. That sounds so deliciously rude, it tempts me. What would it do, Panama?

JOE. Soften and fuzz the image.

ALICE. No, I couldn't be a party to deceit. Honesty regardless has always been my motto.

JOE. I go along with that.

ALICE. Cheers!

(PEGGY gets up and looks out of patio doors.)

PEGGY. That is the Great Man's studio at the end of the garden, isn't it?

NED. No, it was Matthew Hogan's.

ALICE. Yes it is Peggy, and take no notice of Ned, long ago he used to be an art critic.

PEGGY. Why did you stop?

NED. Let's say I was finally battered into submission by

an avalanche of second rate work.

PEGGY. Where did you class Hogan?

NED. Some way below his present reputation. Butch Art Nouveau sums him up. He was a good sculptor, technically excellent but he was also a selfish, expansive, talented cunt and ultimately that shows through in all his work.

(Pause.)

ALICE. There now and I always thought it was my private parts that were most prominently featured.

PEGGY. He was an absolute genius. Posterity will forever remember him for his treatment of hair... head hair, I mean.

(JOE chokes on his orange juice. ALICE smiles at him.)

NED. How boring we're back to Alice's infamous tresses again. Don't you find it trivial Miss Black that a reputation should rest upon a hank of hair?

PEGGY. No, I don't. And the better critics agree with me.

ALICE. I should think so. My hair was very special. Do you know, it was so long I could kneel on it quite easily.

NED. And if anyone knows of a more pointless exercise, I'd be happy to hear of it.

ALICE. That's enough Ned, it is my birthday.

JOE. Congratulations.

ALICE. Thank you.

PEGGY. There's a coincidence... it's Joseph's birthday too.

ALICE. Is it really?

JOE. Er... yes.

ALICE. You don't seem too sure.

JOE. Yes, I am. Just that flying to London, I've lost all track of time.

(JOE exchanges a quick look with a pleased PEGGY.)

ALICE. How marvelous, Panama. I must find something to give you as a present.

NED. A canal would be nice... or a hat?

ALICE. Your head on a plate wouldn't be bad. *(She has been searching the room. She finds a small passe partout framed drawing from the shelves and gives it to JOE.)* Ah, here we are. Perfect. Happy Birthday!

NED. Do we have to sing?

JOE. It's beautiful.

ALICE. Better than a photograph.

(PEGGY goes to look.)

PEGGY. What is it?

JOE. A drawing of Alice.

PEGGY. By Matthew Hogan.

JOE. It is! Look, I can't accept this.

ALICE. Of course you can, the attic's so stuffed with old sketch books it's a fire hazard.

JOE. I'm embarrassed, it's too valuable.

NED. What rubbish, it's not a Matisse, far from it. Hogan was a very poor draftsman.

ALICE. I insist. Same birthday means we're practically related.

JOE. I really appreciate it. Thank you.

ALICE. Good. Now you can do me a favor.

JOE. Name it.

ALICE. Take some photographs of the studio. It would be nice to have a record for sentiment's sake.

JOE. I'd be happy to.

ALICE. Thank you. Be an angel and show him where everything is, Ned.

(NED nods. JOE picks up his camera bag and they begin to go to the patio doors.)

NED. This way. Key still in the flowerpot?

ALICE. Yes and watch yourselves, it's filthy. I'm about to have the whole place gutted and redecorated.

(PEGGY explodes.)

PEGGY. You're going to destroy Matthew Hogan's studio!!

ALICE. It's hardly the burning of the library at Alexandria.

PEGGY. But it's still a monstrous wanton vandalism.

ALICE. There's virtually nothing in there—the odd plinth, a load of dust and his working tools, that's all.

PEGGY. It should be kept for the nation. Anything else is sacrilege.

ALICE. Young lady, I have no intention of living in a shrine. The blue plaque by the front door's quite enough, thank you.

NED. You could always throw it open to the public Wednesday afternoons and serve cream teas.

PEGGY. I'm sorry, it's... it's none of my business. I apologize. I was astonished, that's all.

NED. Mere curiosity, Alice but what do you intend to use it for?

ALICE. Playing ping pong. I can get a full size table in there.

NED. Ask a silly question. Follow me, Mr. Panama.

(NED exits into garden, followed by JOE. ALICE watches them then goes and sits on the chesterfield.)

ALICE. No one believes the truth anymore. You look ill at ease, Miss Black. Do take a seat. *(PEGGY sits in chair and tightlipped begins to unfasten her attache case.)* I hope you're reaching for a lipstick or some item of personal hygiene because I have an aversion to forms and questionnaires.

PEGGY. I'm not here to interview you, Mrs. Hogan, merely to attempt to persuade you to authorize a biography of your late husband.

ALICE. You could do it without my permission and probably will.

PEGGY. One would be foolish to do Leonardo da Vinci without trying for the cooperation of the Mona Lisa.

ALICE. Oh please!

PEGGY. I'm sorry?

ALICE. Go ahead, surprise me.

(PEGGY pulls out two books which she passes over to ALICE.)

PEGGY. These are our most recent best selling biographies.

(ALICE takes them and places them on table behind sofa without a glance.)

ALICE. Thanks, I enjoy a good read.

PEGGY. If any of those authors meet with your approval, we could be in business.

ALICE. I don't think so.

PEGGY. Alternatively, we could use a ghost writer. Someone to do the professional work and you would merely have to reminisce into a tape recorder.

ALICE. Sounds horrific.

PEGGY. Perhaps you would care to nominate a possible writer, someone we could both be happy with?

ALICE. The Marquis de Sade or Jackie Collins—it hardly matters

PEGGY. Most people would consider it selfish to deny the world a further insight into a great man's life. Think how little we know about Shakespeare.

ALICE. Doesn't appear to have harmed his reputation.

PEGGY. Friends and relatives are sometimes wary of unearthing old scandals, rattling skeletons. I want you to know that at Harvest House we treasure our reputation, our last involvement in a libel action occurred way back in 1969 and we won that one.

ALICE. Sounds a sterile organization. Hogan used to say, 'If it offends no one, it stinks.'

(PEGGY quietly leans back, closes her attache case and places it beside her.)

PEGGY. Mrs. Hogan, why are you so hostile towards this project?

ALICE. Because Hogan would have hated it. He was a great believer in letting the work speak for itself. Can you honestly say that it would make any difference if he was suddenly to be revealed as a one-legged, alcoholic homosexual?

PEGGY. I never heard Hogan was gay...

ALICE. You see, it's sheer nosiness. No, I'm sorry. On all counts I must decline.

(PEGGY picks up her case and stands.)

PEGGY. That's a great shame and disappointment. Especially as the other parties I've approaches have been most helpful.

ALICE. Really?

PEGGY. Yes, positively enthusiastic.

ALICE. Name one.

PEGGY. Edith Hogan, she's given me great deal of early material.

ALICE. *(Amazed.)* Edith!! You've actually seen and spoken with Edith Hogan?

PEGGY. OH yes, many times.

ALICE. How amazing, half a lifetime ago she literally vanished off the face of the earth. Sit down. *(PEGGY does so.)* How is Edith? Is she well? Happy?

PEGGY. She's dead. Passed over to the other side.

(Pause.)

ALICE. God, I knew there was something strange about you. How does she contact you, automatic writing, through Big Chief Red Could or is it the blinding light and a small, clear voice in the back of your head? *(She angrily goes to get another drink.)* You show an unexpected lack of ambition, young lady. Why not establish celestial contact with Hogan direct?

PEGGY. Edith Hogan remarried, was widowed, had a good life and died three months ago. I had my meetings with her earlier in the year.

ALICE. Oh, sorry. It was a shock. Glad to hear things worked out for her, Edith was good to me.

PEGGY. She spoke well of you too.

ALICE. Where was she living?

PEGGY. She divided her time between Boston and Geneva, she married money the second time. I have recordings, photostats of all her diaries and witnessed authorization to publish.

ALICE. She must have changed a lot, she didn't used to be naive. I don't see you have a problem Miss Black, you have your book.

PEGGY. It's only half the story.

ALICE. The works of Art are fully documented, the personal stuff I'm sure you can ferret out or invent, it doesn't matter.

PEGGY. It matters to me. I admire Matthew Hogan's work immensely. I'd like to do justice to his life.

ALICE. The work was the most important part of his life.

(ALICE moves away. PEGGY follows her.)

PEGGY. My chief editor was intrigued by certain references to the Hogan sex diaries.

(ALICE stops, turns and snarls.)

ALICE. Not a chance. Forget it.

PEGGY. I find it hard to understand you, Mrs. Hogan. Most people would feel obligated and proud to have shared their life with a genius. Instead you plan to destroy his workplace, allow others to denigrate his talent and blindly strive to conceal his life. Why murder someone after their death?

ALICE. *(Quietly.)* You're an insulting bitch. For thirty years I loved and worshipped that man through every waking moment. But a man not a god, a man. Now go!

(ALICE turns her back on PEGGY.)

PEGGY. May I see the studio? You owe me that at least.

ALICE. One look and out. *(PEGGY exits quickly through patio doors. ALICE sits at her desk and hold her head in her hands.)* God rest your soul, Edith.

(After a moment JOE enters from garden beginning to pack his camera in the bag.)

JOE. Are you okay?

ALICE. Fine.

JOE. You sure?

ALICE. Yes, just a little emotional moment. Are you finished in the studio?

JOE. I shot three rolls, I hope you'll be pleased. Not much in there but it's a beautiful space with fantastic vibes.

ALICE. That was Hogan.

JOE. Reminded me of my boathouse in Maine.

ALICE. You like the sea?

JOE. Boats are my passion... and my great escape.

ALICE. I prefer the shore, I should have been a beachcomber.

JOE. Alice...

ALICE. Yes?

JOE. I'd like to show my appreciation for the drawing. Would you have dinner with me tonight? Please?

ALICE. Not a good idea, I think.

JOE. Just the two of us. The birthday people.

ALICE. No Peggy Black?

JOE. Oh, come on. We want to enjoy ourselves, don't we?

ALICE. I don't know if Ned has any plans to...

JOE. He's going to the theatre, he told me. So?

ALICE. Alright. Thank you Panama.

JOE. That's great. Shall I pick you up around seven?

ALICE. You don't have to do this.

JOE. I know but I want to. Also, I have a proposition I'd like to put to you.

ALICE. I'm getting wary again.

JOE. No need, I'm pretty sure you'll find it amusing.

ALICE. I hope so, I could do with a giggle.

JOE. Did you finish the business with Peggy?

ALICE. Completely. You and she aren't...

JOE. Christ no! I barely know her.

ALICE. I should keep it like that.

JOE. She's an unhappy woman.

ALICE. Brought it on herself, I shouldn't wonder.

JOE. You and she didn't exactly hit it off.

ALICE. I can't remember disliking anyone so much on sight in my life.

JOE. It happens. Don't let it worry you.

ALICE. I won't. This day has certainly stirred up a bundle of memories.

(They look at each other and smile. JOE looks out into the garden.)

JOE. Here they come now. See you at seven.
ALICE. I won't forget.

(NED and PEGGY enter. PEGGY picks up her attache case.)

PEGGY. Thank you for letting me see it. It's beautiful, I do beg you to reconsider your plans.
ALICE. Your concern is noted. Sorry I couldn't be of more help. Good-bye. Can you see yourself out. *(PEGGY exits quickly.)* Good-bye Panama, nice meeting you.
JOE. Same here and thanks again for the drawing. Bye Ned, look after yourself.
NED. Yes indeed. Au revoir.

(JOE exits. Front door bangs.)

ALICE. Thank God for that.
NED. An ill-matched pair.
ALICE. He's lovely, she's vile.
NED. A big Hogan worshipper, she practically genuflected in the studio.
ALICE. Cow. I don't trust her, I shall put the burglar alarm on tonight.
NED. Do I gather that the book is off?
ALICE. As far as I'm concerned, completely.
NED. Poor little Mz Black, so it's back to the Charm School for her.
ALICE. I'm going to have a bath. *(At door.)* Oh, she did

give me one extraordinary piece of news. She saw Edith several times without having to dig up the back garden.

(ALICE exits. NED goes to look at the garden.)

NED. It was just a theory.

(CURTAIN.)

Scene 2

(ALICE enters with a vase half filled with water which she places on table behind sofa. She wears a discreet, expensive dress. Picks up perfume atomizer, squirts a burst on her wrist, then with finger puts some behind her ears, a moment's thought and she dabs a little between her breasts. She tidies the room as a carriage clock begins to strike seven and immediately after in tempo the doorbell rings and she exits. Pause.)

ALICE. *(V.O.)* Hello again. Come in.
JOE. *(V.O.)* Hi, these are for you.
ALICE. *(V.O.)* Thank you, they're lovely. *(ALICE re-enters carrying small bunch of flowers followed by JOE in light trousers, tie and dark jacket.)* You're unbelievably punctual, Panama.
JOE. Habit. It's an important part of my job.

(ALICE has gone straight to vase, tearing off paper from flower stems and placing them in.)

ALICE. There, all prepared. I knew you'd bring flowers.

JOE. Am I that predictable?

ALICE. No just well mannered. I guessed you'd wear a tie as well. Now, what would you like to—of course, you don't.

JOE. No.

ALICE. You must have a beautiful liver.

JOE. That's a first. No one's ever commented on that before.

ALICE. Mineral water? Orange juice?

JOE. No thanks, I'm fine.

ALICE. I won't either. I'll hit the wine with my birthday dinner. Do sit down.

(They both sit.)

JOE. Yes, where would you like to go? I haven't booked anywhere because I didn't want to make a mistake—you know, some place you'd hate.

ALICE. There's a nice Italian restaurant down the road, no need to book they know me all too well.

JOE. Good.

ALICE. How's the censorious Miss Black?

JOE. I haven't seen her since this afternoon. She lay down with a migraine.

ALICE. How exciting, my evil spell worked.

JOE. *(Laughs.)* She disapproves of me too.

ALICE. What a fool! That's enough about her let's talk about something more cheerful—tell me about your proposition.

JOE. Tricky. I don't know if it still applies.

ALICE. Why not?

JOE. Well, I gather that you've turned down the Harvest House idea for a book on Hogan.

ALICE. Yes completely.

JOE. I was sort of part of that deal.

ALICE. Oh, I'm sorry. Of course you were going to take the photographs.

JOE. Not exactly. I was the sweetener, I guess.

ALICE. The what?

JOE. The sweetener, the persuader who breaks down a client's resistance.

ALICE. With violence?

JOE. No. With sex.

(ALICE stares at him with a half smile.)

ALICE. You're joking?... no? No, you're not. Ha! How strange.

JOE. I'm your special offer.

ALICE. My non-returnable free gift?

JOE. You got it.

ALICE. I see. How extraordinary. I will have a drink. *(ALICE goes and pours herself a vodka, turns and sips, looking at JOE.)* You are rotten. I do think you might have spoken up sooner. I could have fobbed Miss Black off for a couple of days—flung in a few maybe's and I'd like to think it over's.

JOE. There's still time.

ALICE. No, I practically threw her out of the house, she'd smell a rat for sure.

JOE. Seems a waste—I'm all paid for.

(ALICE returns to her seat.)

ALICE. Do Harvest House keep you under a long term contract?

JOE. No, I gather this was entirely Miss Black's idea, a one time deal for me. Most of the time I'm self employed.

ALICE. I see, you're a freelance fucker.

JOE. That's about the size of it.

(Pause.)

ALICE. Why are you telling me all this?

JOE. Because I don't seduce. I consider it ammoral.

ALICE. Doesn't that cramp your style somewhat?

JOE. Would you believe this is the first time the question has come up? Normally, it's a straightforward above board business transaction with no hassles.

ALICE. Fascinating.

JOE. So, that's my proposition. Are you going to look a gift horse in the mouth? *(ALICE opens her mouth to speak then doesn't.)* It's entirely up to you.

ALICE. For once in my life, Mr. Panama, I don't know what to say.

JOE. I'll understand if you object on moral grounds.

ALICE. With my past reputation that's pretty unlikely.

JOE. Maybe... I don't appeal to you?

ALICE. You know damn well you do.

JOE. So?

ALICE. So. I'm thinking.

(Pause.)

JOE. You'd also be doing me a big favor, Alice.

ALICE. *(Mildly flattered.)* I would?

JOE. Yes, I get a special big bonus if I lay you.

(ALICE gets up.)

ALICE. Finally, we get town to the nitty gritty, you mercenary bastard.

(JOE gets up and follows her.)

JOE. No please, forget I said that. I already have my standard fee plus expenses, I like you a lot, so let's go and eat.

ALICE. Wait. She doesn't need to know you struck out. I'm perfectly willing to sign an invoice or delivery note for you.

JOE. I really appreciate you offering but it wouldn't be ethical. I couldn't live with it.

ALICE. How much is the bonus?

JOE. A thousand dollars.

ALICE. That much!

JOE. I could get a new sail for my boat, I've been saving up.

ALICE. Aaaaaahhhh! Come over here. *(She gestures to him, he goes to her.)* Kiss me. *(They exchange a long, lingering kiss, and she finally pulls away.)* I'll split the bonus with you 50/50.

JOE. You're not serious?

ALICE. I most certainly am. Do we have ourselves a deal?

JOE. You want five hundred dollars to... to screw me?

ALICE. Yes, fair division of labor. And don't worry, Panama,

I'll earn my whack.

JOE. Well, I hope this doesn't start a new trend but you're on. Shake. *(They shake hands smiling.)* You are something special, Alice. I'm going to buy you the best meal you ever had.

ALICE. I have a confession to make.

JOE. What's that?

(She starts undoing his tie.)

ALICE. I never have been able to resist opening my presents immediately.

(CURTAIN.)

END OF ACT I

ACT II

Scene 1

(The following morning. Light filtering through drawn curtains. ALICE wearing a towelling robe enters with a mug of coffee and a glass of orange juice which she puts down on table. She draws back the curtains and sits on sofa and sips her coffee.
JOE enters in white towelling robe.)

JOE. This feels good and it's my size.

ALICE. I'm very organized, I get them wholesale.

JOE. And toothbrushes?

ALICE. Those too, by the gross. Have your orange juice first.

JOE. Great. *(He sits and drinks. ALICE pensively sips her coffee.)* You're very quiet this morning.

ALICE. I've been having, 'situations one never imagined to find oneself in' thoughts.

JOE. Ah.

ALICE. Is your usual standard fee very high?

JOE. Yes. I'm in my prime.

47

ALICE. Whatever the market will stand, eh? Still, there are threads of sadness and waste about it all.

JOE. You mean, 'What's a nice guy like me doing in a place like this?

ALICE. Something along those lines. Boring question, I suppose?

JOE. I've been there before. It's simple. I tried a lot of different, regular jobs till I was 24, didn't seem to be getting anywhere special, so I took stock and decided I had this natural, God given gift which it would be a crime not to use. It's worked out fine.

ALICE. How old are you now?

JOE. 31, that's why I can handle it. A teenager would be wiped out.

ALICE. It's got to be a short career, though.

JOE. Like an athlete. I plan to retire in a couple of years or so.

ALICE. Then what?

JOE. I've been careful, saved a few dollars, invested in bonds and own a half share in a boatyard. I'll probably sail the seven seas and see what turns up.

ALICE. Sounds idyllic if short sighted.

JOE. Who can rely on tomorrow being there?

ALICE. I'm still curious. Hasn't the moral aspect of it ever worried you?

JOE. No, did it bother you?

ALICE. I'm sorry?

JOE. Last night. You screwed for money—half my big bonus.

ALICE. Oh! That was a joke, I never intended to...

JOE. You're very generous, thanks Alice.

ALICE. Seriously though, no doubts, anxieties or hang ups?

JOE. No, it's a talent like any other and the beauty of it is it's honest and in the open. I'm not a fortune hunter, nobody has to give me expensive jewelry and I'm good value.

ALICE. True. But I still don't see where you find all these rich, desperate women.

JOE. You've got the wrong idea, they aren't desperate. The majority of my clients are career women who run business empires. My timing was so lucky you wouldn't believe it, I came in on the wave of the whole Feminist explosion. Some of them get a real buzz from paying me for it, it's like they're exacting a two thousand year revenge for their exploited sisters. The rest are just too busy and they welcome my sensible solution to their problem.

ALICE. Too busy for sex? That's a new one.

JOE. Listen, sex is so time consuming for a single woman in Western Society. First she has to find a man, then even if she decides to put out on a first date, there's the hairdressing appointment, the manicure, the make-up, decisions on what to wear, straighten up the apartment, change the sheets, the towels, wax her legs, check her periods, her articles of contraception, her breath, her armpits. Finally, HE arrives. And what happens? Action? No. There's the drinks, the chit chat, the theatre or the movie, the restaurant, the talk. When he takes her back to her place hours or it can seem like weeks later, she is exhausted. She longs for bed—to sleep. But she has committed herself, so now it's lucky draw time. He won't stop yacking about his wife, his guilt, his work. He confesses he's gay and wants her to help, he's too rough or too gentle, he's 'strange' and she doesn't have the right kind of boots. He's got performance problems, he's too quick, too slow or he can't

quite make it and she gets humped into a coma. And this you
have to realize is a hardworking woman who has to be at her
office first thing in the morning.

ALICE. Poor thing will have a nervous breakdown if she
carries on like that. What is she to do?

JOE. Help is at hand. She calls up Panamaman. Makes an
appointment, quick shower, Joseph arrives promptly. One hour
later she feels real good, no tensions. She can catch up on her
paperwork, learn a foreign language, or just relax with friends
and watch T.V. She is free. I take all major credit cards, she
can swing it on expenses.

ALICE. You're a good salesman. But what about romance?

JOE. Joseph Conrad quote, 'Romance is like the horizon'.

ALICE. And dare I say it, Love?

JOE. That joker's wild, cancels out everything I've said.
But you can die waiting for it to happen.

ALICE. Maybe I should set up as your London agent. I
used to have a talent for procuring and loads of experience.

JOE. So I heard, Peggy filled me in about Hogan. I'd love
to read the sex diaries.

ALICE. I'll lend you 'The Aspern Papers' by Henry James,
you'll find that more interesting.

JOE. I think I've read it.

ALICE. I'm bloody sure Peggy has.

(NED enters with a small wrapped package in his hand.)

NED. Oh, you are up. I've been pussyfooting around trying not to disturb you. Good morning, Joseph.

JOE. How you doing, Ned?

NED. Fine. Are you arriving early or leaving late?

JOE. I stayed the night.

NED. Strange, I didn't feel the earth move.

ALICE. We had a smashing double birthday treat. What's that you're cuddling in your crotch?

NED. Special delivery. I noticed the chic, black van draw up and intercepted it.

(He hands package to ALICE who tears the wrapping off.)

ALICE. Fabulous a late present.

NED. Maybe I should warn you...

(ALICE stops opening the cardboard carton.)

ALICE. It's not...?

NED. *(Nods.)* Gloria, or what is left of her.

ALICE. It looks awfully small, Ned. Are you sure?

NED. My dear, I saw the van and I doubt that they deliver by installments.

ALICE. We still don't have a scattering location.

NED. I thought you had decided on the Savoy Grill?

ALICE. I went off that idea. I know it's a pointless exercise but I somehow think there ought to be trees and flowers.

NED. Derry and Toms roof garden.

ALICE. Too windy.

NED. St. James's Park then.

ALICE. Too many ducks. Sorry Panama, this was a dear friend of ours.

JOE. Right. Think I'll go get dressed. Leave you to it.

(JOE exits.)

NED. Well, well, well. So much for chastity.

ALICE. It was a totally new, extraordinary experience I couldn't possibly pass up.

NED. You do surprise me.

ALICE. Meaning you were convinced there was nothing I hadn't already done?

NED. That too. But my thoughts were on Mr. Panama, he strikes one as a pleasantly straightforward creature, hardly an innovator and certainly not the Einstein of the mattress that you seem to suggest.

ALICE. The actual act was faultless, highly professional and so it ought to be, the man's a prostitute.

NED. Let me get this straight, is he what my generation would call a gigolo?

ALICE. No, nothing like. He's encased in so many rules and regulations as to make a trade union seem flexible. He doesn't flash his teeth, walk the dog or dance the tango. He's a completely new breed, he just bangs by the hour.

NED. You're mad, he must have cost you a small fortune or is there a special cheap rate during the night like the telephones?

ALICE. He's... what was it he called it?... a sweetener, a gift, an inducement courtesy of the American publishers and the repellent Miss Black.

NED. A bribe.

ALICE. Yes. The odd thing is that Panama himself is nice, very very nice.

NED. He reminds you of Hogan, you've always had a fatal weakness for big Americans.

ALICE. It's not that simple. He's somehow extra simpatico.

NED. So now I presume you've stupidly obligated yourself to render assistance in the compilation of this boring biography?

ALICE. No, I haven't signed anything, I've merely taken advantage. And there's a unique aspect to this kind of bribe.

NED. What's that?

ALICE. It's virtually impossible to give it back.

(Doorbell rings.)

NED. I'll go, it may be more of Gloria. *(He exits quickly. ALICE undoes the cardboard carton and takes out a cremation jar, which she hold in both hands and lightly kisses. NED returns.)* Surprise, surprise. Peggy Black with a posy of flowers.

ALICE. Shit!

NED. Do you want to see her?

ALICE. No. Wait, I think I'd better after last night. Where is she?

NED. I shoved her in the study.

ALICE. Where she's busy whizzing through my private correspondence no doubt. Keep your eye on her while I go and throw some clothes on.

(Exiting she hands him the jar.)

NED. What's this?

ALICE. Instant Gloria.

(She exits. NED places jar on table behind sofa and exits briefly.)

NED. *(V.O.)* Do come into the living room, Miss Black.

(NED holds door open for PEGGY to enter carrying posy.)

NED. Alice shouldn't be long, she's getting dressed.

PEGGY. Oh! I didn't want to take a chance on missing her.

NED. And you haven't... by at least three hours. Alice seldom ventures out before noon.

(PEGGY puts posy down on desk and wanders round the room. NED perches on sofa arm and watches her.)

PEGGY. I didn't sleep at all last night.

NED. Ah, what it is to be young.

PEGGY. I wish yesterday had never happened. My whole approach to Mrs. Hogan was so gross, I get nauseous just thinking about it. My problem is that this project has become so important to me that I tend to over react. Can you understand that?

NED. Absolutely. I myself only harbor strong feelings about trivia.

PEGGY. How long have you known Mrs. Hogan?

NED. Since she was sixteen. I introduced her to Hogan, he was looking for a new model and Alice was extraordinary at that age.

PEGGY. So she moved in and took over?

NED. No, after a while she began living here, that's all. Then they fell in love and Alice was lost—the rest of her life devoted to Hogan and that was no easy task, believe you me.

PEGGY. She seems well able to take care of herself now.

NED. She learned how to cope, she was forced to by love and circumstances.

PEGGY. When the first Mrs. Hogan walked out?

NED. Yes, that was a mystery. I gather you met Edith before she died?

PEGGY. Many times.

NED. I liked Edith, nothing fazed her. I always pictured her as one of those pioneer women on a wagon train rolling West, giving birth with one hand and killing an Apache with the other. Wholly admirable.

PEGGY. The reality was she ended her days in a lakeside mansion in Geneva with ten bedrooms, a customized Rolls Royce station wagon and two tennis courts.

NED. Two seems excessive.

PEGGY. One hard, one grass.

NED. Edith did have style. How did it happen? Did she strike oil?

PEGGY. She struck a multi-millionaire who died five years later.

NED. How amazing! I do enjoy hearing about other people's lives, it makes up for the lack of my own.

PEGGY. That could be an advantage.

NED. In what way?

PEGGY. Prevents you getting hurt.

NED. Proxy emotions can be devastating, I suffer through my friends.

PEGGY. Why did you hate Matthew Hogan?

NED. It was a game we both played, a game based on particles of truth. I enjoy games, don't you?

PEGGY. Only when I win.

NED. That requires a conviction I don't possess. Are you based in New York?

PEGGY. Yes, my work is there.

NED. But you're not a native?
PEGGY. No, I'm from Boston.
NED. Ah, that explains a lot.
PEGGY. Such as what?
NED. Your ... accent for one.

(JOSEPH enters in last night's clothes without tie and carry-
ing jacket. He's surprised to see PEGGY.)

JOE. Peggy! Hi!
PEGGY. Good morning, Joseph.
JOE. How're you doing?
PEGGY. Fine.

(An awkward silence which NED breaks by gathering up the
mug, glass and packaging.)

NED. I may as well earn my keep.
JOE. Do you need some help, Ned?
NED. Thank you but I do most things better by myself.

(He exits with JOSEPH holding door open for him and clos-
ing it after.)

PEGGY. I wondered where you'd got to.
JOE. Aren't you going to congratulate me?
PEGGY. You did it?
JOE. Sure thing, went like a dream. Congress took place, I
didn't seduce and you owe me a thousand bucks.
PEGGY. That's perfect, changes everything.
JOE. Don't get your hopes up too high. You're not exactly

flavor of the month with Alice. In fact, she hates your guts.

PEGGY. Good. Publishing is a cut-throat business, no room for sentiment. *(She takes check book from her purse and sits at desk.)* I'll write you out a check right away.

JOE. No hurry, I trust you.

PEGGY. I prefer to settle all my accounts promptly. Did you stick to all your stupid rules?

JOE. Every single one.

PEGGY. No family talk? No personal stuff? You were here all night.

JOE. The subject never came up.

PEGGY. Payment in full, Mr. Panama. You've earned it.

(PEGGY holds out check. JOE takes it, looks at it and folds it into his back pocket.)

JOE. Thanks.

PEGGY. You will now go to the hotel, pack your bags and get the next flight back, fast.

JOE. Hold on, I plan on staying a while, you know see the town, take in Stratford, Windsor, the works.

PEGGY. You can't this time around. Get going will you.

JOE. I intend to take a little vacation, Miss Black. I need a break, so up yours.

PEGGY. Listen asshole, I don't give a damn where you go, Paris, Rome or Timbuktu just as long as you get out of England. Do I make myself clear?

JOE. Hey, what is this?

PEGGY. Our business arrangement is concluded and I'm telling you to get the hell out of here. Now!

JOE. Tough. You've got me curious, I'm staying.

PEGGY. Think about it most carefully, Joseph. It'll cost you *(JOE's hand goes to his back pocket.)* and it isn't worth it.

JOE. You'd cancel the check?

PEGGY. *(Nods.)* All I want is to feel clean again.

JOE. Oh, Guilt! You should've said, that's your problem entirely. I'll do as you say, be in Paris for lunch. *(He pulls on his jacket.)* I'll just be a couple of minutes...

PEGGY. No, go immediately.

JOE. Don't I even get to be polite and say good-bye to Alice and Ned?

PEGGY. I'll make your excuses. Send them a postcard. Bye.

JOE. Jesus!

(JOE exits. PEGGY quickly rummages in her purse, finds bottle of pills, takes two, chokes and goes to drinks. Picks up brandy bottle, can't find glass so takes a quick swig from bottle as NED enters. She sees him and coughs putting down bottle.)

NED. Bless you.

PEGGY. Sorry, I had to take some medicine.

NED. I understand, I've got an aunt puts away a bottle a day to keep her arthritis at bay. Actually, I heard the door slam and thought you'd taken umbrage and left.

PEGGY. That was Joseph. There was a telex at the hotel, the company wants him back in New York.

NED. So soon? It's like crossing the Atlantic by yo-yo.

PEGGY. He's used to sudden assignments. Part of the game.

(ALICE enters dressed in casuals.)

ALICE. Good morning Miss Black.

PEGGY. Good morning, it's so good of you to see me. *(PEGGY picks up posy and gives it to ALICE.)* I brought you these.

ALICE. Thank you. *(She hands posy to NED.)* Put them in the kitchen, will you Ned? I won't be long.

NED. Certainly.

(NED exits. ALICE sits, composed and chilly. PEGGY looks about to speak but doesn't. Pause.)

ALICE. How can I help you?

PEGGY. I'm sorry, during the night I prepared and memorized a speech of abject apology and now I can't recall a single word.

ALICE. Then 'sorry' will have to do.

PEGGY. Mrs. Hogan, my behavior yesterday was unforgivable.

ALICE. You were disappointed and frustrated, that's a perfect recipe for anger.

PEGGY. You have such rare gifts of perception and understanding.

ALICE. Don't overdo it, Miss Black. I haven't and I won't be changing my mind about publication.

PEGGY. *(Smiles.)* Can't win them all.

ALICE. If it's any consolation, Hogan's sex diary is a complete non event. I comprises of long lists written in a childish code, setting down ages, positions and frequency of orgasm. About as erotic as a small boy's collection of car registration numbers.

PEGGY. I see. Does he award points on a scale of one to ten?

ALICE. He uses stars.

PEGGY. Really? And how many stars would you give to Joe Panama?

ALICE. Ah, thank goodness you reminded me. My dear, I was about to write you a thank you note, it's on my list of things to do.

PEGGY. Was he up to your standard?

ALICE. Yes, delightful. A little too accomplished perhaps, there were moments when I felt as if I were some weird product being whizzed along an assembly line for final packaging. But all in all a memorable experience and worth every penny of your money.

PEGGY. He told you.

ALICE. Yes. I gather he refuses to seduce.

PEGGY. And you don't mind?

ALICE. Quite the contrary, I shall dine out on the story in the louche circles I frequent.

PEGGY. I'm glad. Funny thing is, the story's even better than you think.

ALICE. Really?

PEGGY. There's something you don't know.

ALICE. Not hidden cameras? I've always longed to be a film star.

PEGGY. Nothing so dramatic, just that Joseph Panama is the son of Matthew Hogan. (*ALICE endures a moment of genuine shock then bursts out into laughter.*) I don't suppose it's a 'first' for you, screwing the father and the son.

ALICE. It's the most ludicrous thing I've ever heard. And thank God, impossible—Hogan had no children.

PEGGY. I checked it out most carefully and there's no doubt.

ALICE. Hogan suffered two paternity claims against him in his life, both were dismissed out of court on irrefutable evidence.

PEGGY. This is the truth.

ALICE. Alas, it's an all too common delusion, imagining yourself to be the illegitimate offspring of a famous person.

PEGGY. Joseph Panama himself doesn't know and he's perfectly legitimate. Edith Hogan was still married to Hogan at the time of his birth.

ALICE. Are you saying that Edith was his mother?

PEGGY. Yes and her second husband Stefan Panama adopted the year old baby.

ALICE. Are you sure of this?

PEGGY. Absolutely. I'm a meticulous researcher.

ALICE. It could explain why she left without a word... Hogan was too selfish to tolerate a child in the household, disrupting his work and routine... but... no, I find it impossible to believe, Edith was always faithful.

PEGGY. I'm bewildered. According to Edith Hogan's records you were there at the time of birth.

ALICE. That settles it, the whole thing's a sham, utter madness. Was she senile towards the end?

PEGGY. I found her very bright. *(PEGGY takes out notebook from her purse.)* I made some notes from her diary... yes, here we are. 14th of July, Brendon Cottage, Kingston St. Mary, Somerset. *(She looks up and watches ALICE.)* PM after a difficult labor, my darling Joseph born. Midwife and Alice present.

(ALICE has turned to stone.)

ALICE. *(In a whisper.)* No... no... they said it was dead...
dead.
PEGGY. What are you saying? I can't hear you, Alice.

(ALICE shatters and screams.)

ALICE. THEY SAID THE BABY WAS DEAD. IT WAS
MINE! It was born dead. Dead I,-------

*(ALICE begins to retch and staggers into the garden like a
    wounded bird and retches violently. PEGGY watches her
    with cold serenity. NED enters quickly.)*

NED. What's happened? I heard shouting.
PEGGY. Alice seems upset. She just found out she's a
mother.

*(NED gives her an amazed glance then seeing ALICE in the
    garden runs to help her. PEGGY slowly leaves the room,
    looking back as if to memorize the scene. She exits. NED
    supports a shrunken ALICE back into the room, places her
    in a chair and hurriedly gets a drink which he forces to her
    lips.)*

NED. Take a sip. Go on. That's it. *(ALICE swallows some
then pushes it away. NED takes his handkerchief and gently
wipes her face of tears. Hands her hanky.)* Blow your nose.
Hard.

(ALICE does so. Still breathless, she looks around.)

ALICE. Where's that bitch?

NED. Never mind her, she's gone. How are you?

ALICE. In pieces... Edith said the baby was dead, Ned, I swear... born dead... best to forget... And, Aah!...

NED. I'm not very good at hitting people, my love, so don't force me to slap you. Let it all pour out, tell me. *(She grips his hand ferociously.)* Come on, can't be that bad.

ALICE. So long ago, it doesn't seem real. I was eighteen... another person. Model, mistress and still madly in love with Hogan but I'd adjusted to the situation... thought it very adult and sophisticated... discovering life... much sought after... then, I got pregnant. Edith was marvelous, took charge, talked me out of an abortion... made all the arrangements.

NED. Arrangements for what? Adoption?

ALICE. Yes, we told no one. Edith rented a place in Somerset and came to visit when she could. She stayed by me all the time I was in labor... that was an endless nightmare... I was out of my mind with pain. My next memory is Edith telling me the baby was stillborn... that I was to forget and concentrate on getting well again. So I did... it was a relief, I didn't want my life to change in any way. And now... now, that vile creature tells me Edith took the child, raised it as her own and... and it's Panama... who... who...

NED. Don't start again, it can't be true.

ALICE. She reeled off all the right dates and addresses, it has to be. Only Edith and the midwife knew, Hogan thought I was visiting my father.

NED. Not to worry, I'll have a word with the interested parties.

ALICE. No, not Panama, no that would be unbearable. He must never know, promise me, please.

NED, Of course, give me credit for some sense.

ALICE. There's one appalling fact I've never admitted to myself.

NED. What?

ALICE. Once in that country cottage, I thought I heard a baby cry... I made myself believe it was my imagination because I was so selfishly in love... only Hogan mattered.

NED. You're still jumping wildly to conclusions.

ALICE. *(Shakes head.)* It's all come together, I can sense it in my bones.

NED. Shall I make us some tea?

ALICE. Ned, it's beyond cups of tea, it's incest! Incest for God's sake!

NED. Calm down, hot tea is supposed to be good for shock.

(ALICE abruptly gets up and moves away.)

ALICE. No... it's no use... this won't last, it will come back.

(NED follows her.)

NED. What will?

ALICE. The panic is there waiting. The monstrosity of it all hasn't fully sunk in... but it will though, I know it will... I wont' be able to get through the night... not with this... never... no more nights. *(She crosses to divan and from under it pulls a small case. She sits on bed and opens case.)* Funny we talked about it yesterday, I'm not usually the premonition type, You will help me, Ned? Stay with me? Hold my hand and place a coin in my mouth?

NED. I'm not letting you out of my sight.

(ALICE hold up a bottle of multi-colored sleeping capsules.)

ALICE. Sixteen does it with half a bottle of vodka.
NED. Give them to me.
ALICE. You mustn't stop me, you're my friend. I beg you.

(NED takes bottle from her hand.)

ALICE. I'll do it sooner or later.
NED. Then we choose later.
ALICE. Ned, this way is clean and sure. Another time I may make the most dreadful hash of it. Please.

(ALICE holds out her hand. NED unscrews bottle and gives her a couple, putting bottle in his pocket.)

NED. You will take two and hopefully shut up for a while. If we get proof positive and if you still want to kill yourself— I'll give you the rest. Now, lie down.

(NED lifts cover for her to lie on divan and makes her comfortable.)

ALICE. There's no point. I know that child lived.
NED. Fine have it your way, wallow in it. Suppose, just suppose it is Panama, are you going to cut him off without a penny? Shouldn't you make a new will, at least? It would certainly alter his life, he could make love for fun in the future. Don't you owe your son that, you selfish cow?
ALICE. I hadn't thought of that.
NED. Yes, a chance at last to show a little maternal concern.

ALICE. But—

NED. No buts. I refuse to let you take the easy way out this time, drifting off in an emotional, alcoholic haze and conveniently ignoring your obligations.

ALICE. If I leave him a fortune, won't he think it awfully strange?

NED. No, of course not. Americans are the world's optimists, they're suckled from birth on fairy tales. He'll accept it as a charming, eccentric, dotty gesture from a charming eccentric, dotty woman. *(He kisses her on the forehead.)* Loosen your stays and make yourself comfy while I get you a glass of water.

(BLACKOUT.)

Scene 2

(ALICE asleep on divan under cover. NED and JOSEPH walk in from garden. They talk in low voices.)

NED. At least it's settled. I'm sorry I had to involve you and make you miss your plane.

JOE. Thank God you got me in time. I still find it hard to believe, it's such a sick thing to do to anyone. I had a gut feeling all along there was something odd about the woman but the travel angle tempted me. It was a chance to do Europe and get paid for it.

NED. If I may say so Joseph, you do have the most extraordinary occupation.

JOE. I don't think so but I can appreciate that others have difficulty in accepting it.

NED. How did you yourself come to terms with it?

JOE. Logically. Once you realize that people pay for most services in life one way or the other, that's the big breakthrough.

NED. Sounds sane when you say it. *(HE looks at ALICE and his watch.)* She's been flat out for three hours. Time I think, to wake her and put her out of her misery.

JOE. I'll go wait outside.

NED. No stay. She's such a suspicious creature she'll think I've made it all up to soothe her. *(JOE has moved to patio window. NED crosses to ALICE and gently wakes her.)* Alice. Time to wake up.

(ALICE slowly turns, wakes, orientates herself. She touches NED's face.)

ALICE. Hello, darling.
NED. How do you feel?

(ALICE sits up.)

ALICE. Rough. And I've had the most appalling dreams.

NED. Yes, well keep them to yourself. Other people's dreams are as boring as their operations. I've got good news.

ALICE. Oh yes?

NED. Joseph Panama is not, repeat not your natural offspring.

ALICE. I was hoping that was one of the nightmares. It's no use Ned, the time, the place, the people, they all fit. My throat is so dry.

(ALICE gets up to move to drinks.)

NED. Alice will you listen carefully for once in your life?

ALICE. Too late for that, too late for every— *(She sees JOSEPH and wheels round on NED.)* You deceitful bastard!

NED. I told you she wouldn't believe me. You try, Joseph.

(JOSEPH hold out his passport to ALICE.)

JOE. It's the truth Alice. Take a look.

ALICE. What's that?

JOE. My passport.

(ALICE takes it gingerly and reads.)

NED. And we haven't had the time or facilities to forge it should that thought cross your mine.

ALICE. Joseph Leopold Panama...

JOE. Born in Berlin.

ALICE. The tenth of January, 1967... it wasn't your birthday yesterday.

JOE. No, that was Peggy's idea. Now we know why.

ALICE. Why Berlin?

JOE. My mother's German, dad was in the army. They are both alive and well and living in Santa Monica. I visit with them every Christmas.

(ALICE half laughs half cries.)

ALICE. What a good son you are.

NED. So, you're convinced?

ALICE. Yes, yes, yes.

NED. Positively? You're not going to insist on blood tests, lie detectors or curiously shaped strawberry marks?

ALICE. No. *(She hugs him.)* Thank you, Ned.

NED. I think we all deserve a drink.

(He goes to drinks. ALICE takes JOSEPH's hand and squeezes it.)

ALICE. Bless you too my lovely Panama.

JOE. It was nothing. I don't agree with folks being set up, another of my rules.

(ALICE drops his hand and switches into an instant high fury gear.)

ALICE. *(Shouts.)* Yes, what about that? Set up! Where is that evil bitch? I can't wait to tear her hair out and kick her in the tit. And why did she do it? Why? *(Kicks sofa.)* Why? *(Flings cushion across room.)* Why? *(Throws GLORIA's urn through open patio windows. She beats sofa with her fists.)* Oh, I'm so angry! I'm livid!

(NED has followed the urn's flight with his eyes. Drink in hand he goes to ALICE.)

NED. Drink this. *(ALICE knocks it back in one.)* Was Gloria fond of your garden?

ALICE. Don't try to change the subject.

NED. Because she happens to be in it now.

ALICE. What do you mean?

(NED takes her hand and leads her to windows. The three of them stare out.)

NED. See. Mainly in the lily bed—the urn broke against the ash tree, wildly appropriate.

ALICE. How did she get there?

NED. You just threw her.

ALICE. My God, I thought it was a vase.

NED. Would you like me to get the hoover out?

ALICE. Don't be silly, Ned. Actually, lilies were her favorite flowers.

NED. That's it then. A truly memorable occasion though I have attended more dignified ceremonies.

ALICE. You are a pig, you know I feel dreadful.

JOE. I'd be very happy if it were me, it's a mighty pretty spot.

ALICE. Thank you, Panama, you are turning out well. *(She lifts her glass in a toast.)* To Gloria, God Bless her!

(NED and JOE murmur 'To Gloria' and they all turn back into the room.)

NED. Two problems solved, one to go.

ALICE. Yes, Miss Peggy Black.

JOE. My guess is she was putting on the pressure for blackmail. She was desperate to get hold of the sex diaries.

ALICE. But I told her they were a dead loss, a list of sterile statistics.

NED. She's obviously obsessed with Hogan, that proves her unbalanced at the very least.

ALICE. Me too, I suppose?

NED. You were in love with him, quite different, you're excused.

ALICE. I'm worried what her next move is going to be. Did she drop any hints, Panama?

JOE. No, she paid me my bonus and told me to get out of town fast. I was kind of hurt.

ALICE. I know, let's all go to the south of France for a couple of weeks. My treat.

NED. That would be running away.

ALICE. Sounds sensible to me. There's a nutter on the loose who hates me and may throw a bomb through the window at any minute. *(Doorbell rings.)* Correction. She's decided to send it through the post.

(NED exits to answer door.)

JOE. I think the best thing I can do is go back to the hotel, wait for Peggy to show up and see if I can get some sense out of her.

ALICE. I feel in jeopardy, that woman has destroyed my confidence.

JOE. Wish I didn't feel so responsible, I'm sorry.

(ALICE kisses him on the cheek.)

ALICE. You're the angel who saved my life. In more ordinary circumstances, I'd be incredibly proud to have you for a son.

JOE. Thanks.

(NED re-enters.)

NED, It's drama time again. You have a visitor.

(He stands aside to let PEGGY enter. She walks in slowly, her appearance is dishevelled, she grips one arm across her chest and gives a strained, half smile.)

ALICE. And what catastrophic news do you bring with you this time?

PEGGY. I... I'm sorry, I have to sit down. *(She staggers slightly into center chair.)* I've been walking in circles ever since I left here. *(Nervous laugh.)* Everyone's present, even Mr. Panama. So, is everything sorted out?... Everything crystal clear?

ALICE. No. Not everything.

PEGGY. Presumably you've worked out that he's not yours and Hogan's son?

ALICE. Yes, and he's not mine and the milkman's either.

PEGGY. Ah, now that's something I never considered. Should've with your track record. Dammit, thought I'd covered all the angles.

ALICE. Before I break your neck, Peggy Black—tell me why you did it.

PEGGY. That's a tough question. I knew this morning, oh, did I! This morning I wanted to spit on your soul. I wanted you in Hell and I wanted to see it.

ALICE. You got your wish.

PEGGY. I know, it was wonderful... for all of five minutes. Now I'm empty—and hurting—and ashamed. I screwed up.

ALICE. Why did you want to punish me? I'm a stranger to you. Why so much hate?

PEGGY. Can't you guess? It wasn't all lies. Edith told the

truth in her journals, she just never told me. I found out when I was going through her papers for probate... an unexpected and unwelcome part of my inheritance.

(Pause.)

    ALICE. My child did live.
    PEGGY. You're so right... *(Tiny laugh.)* Mother.

(ALICE sits on the end of the chesterfield and continues to stare at PEGGY.)

    JOE. We'd better leave you two alone.
    NED. I think I should stay, after all there's—
    ALICE. *(Sharply.)* Ned!
    NED. Yes. Alright.

(NED follows JOSEPH in his exit. The two women remain static, frozen in time.)

    ALICE. Mother... mother.
    PEGGY. Sounds unnatural, doesn't it?
    ALICE. Yes. I'll have to try to get used to it.
    PEGGY. Don't bother, I'll call you Alice.

(Slowly ALICE puts out her hand to PEGGY who takes it and they sit in silence for a while.)

    ALICE. Do you feel anything?
    PEGGY. Some warmth. How about you?
    ALICE. I feel life and it scares me.

PEGGY. Nothing else? Love?

ALICE. No. You?

PEGGY. Negative.

ALICE. We can hardly expect it to be instant in our case.

PEGGY. Maybe never.

(They withdraw their hands.)

ALICE. I hope not... I do hope not. I promise to try, Peggy. It's just that... oh, my head is so full of questions.

PEGGY. I have some of my own to ask. *(She gets up and circles her chair.)* Like how in Hell could you give me away without even holding me?

ALICE. Edith told me the baby was stillborn. You have to believe that, that if nothing else.

PEGGY. And?

ALICE. At the time, it simplified everything, provided an easy solution. I asked no questions. We neither of us mentioned the birth again. Three months later, Edith disappeared form all our lives.

PEGGY. That is so smooth.

ALICE. It's the truth.

PEGGY. The journal tells a different story, how you were hysterical and wanted an abortion, how you only agreed to go through with it on condition that I was put up for immediate adoption. No questions! Yes, that I believe. My God, you didn't even ask what sex I was! That has to be the most total act of denial ever. You were determined to close your heart and mind... to pretend I never happened.

ALICE. Some of that is true... some of it. But we all bend the truth to justify ourselves—even Edith. I can only swear to you that I thought you were dead.

PEGGY. But how could you not ask if it was a boy or a girl? That chilled my spine when I first read it.

ALICE. Please try to understand, it was a long and agonizing birth. Towards the end I was virtually unconscious with pain, then suddenly the nightmare was over, Edith told me the sad result and I didn't have the chance to think again.

PEGGY. And you were glad because you'd never wanted me.

ALICE. At the time, no, I didn't... at the time.

(PEGGY sits. Pause.)

PEGGY. Christ this is difficult. I didn't dream you existed till three months ago.

ALICE. Bear with me then, I've had about three minutes to adjust. Tell me why you wanted revenge. Resentment, curiosity I can understand but why the burning hatred? Where's the harm? Wasn't Edith a good mother, she must have loved you dearly considering what she did, what she sacrificed?

PEGGY. Ha! Yes, she loved me. She drowned me in love, a thick, suffocating love, I was spoiled, protected and crushed by it. When I finally managed to leave home to work in New York, I was twenty five and it felt like I'd won a war. Then the phone calls started. Nightly missiles poisoned with tips of guilt and betrayal that ripped into my guts because I was incapable of hurting her.

ALICE. I see.

PEGGY. I was in analysis for two lousy years. Love is threatening, love is a stranglehold, avoid love, be suspicious of affection. It screwed up all my relationships.

ALICE. I'm sorry. How did you get on with your stepfather?

PEGGY. He died too soon. Edith told me my real father had been killed in a car crash, that he'd been a banker.

ALICE. That was unkind.

PEGGY. I managed to cope but I couldn't with what I read in those notebooks. They wiped me out. My whole existence became a fraud, my father was one of the world's great artists and my mother a...

ALICE. Say it.

PEGGY. A famous model.

ALICE. Thanks.

PEGGY. You were still alive and you'd robbed me of my proper life. Cold bloodedly denied me. I loathed you for that. I *needed* revenge.

ALICE. You certainly got it. *(ALICE stands and moves slightly.)* So. I have a grown up daughter. Amazing.

PEGGY. Any motherly advice?

ALICE. I wouldn't know how.

PEGGY. And no sudden onset of maternal passion?

(ALICE shakes her head and touches PEGGY's shoulder gently.)

ALICE. All I have to offer is regret.

(PEGGY gives a sob and gets up to clutch ALICE in her arms. They remain tightly embraced till ALICE breaks away.)

PEGGY. I'm a mess.

ALICE. You look fine except that your hands are dirty and

there are bits of grass in your hair.

PEGGY. I lay down in a park somewhere.

ALICE. Go and freshen up. I'm all talked out for the moment.

(ALICE steers PEGGY to door.)

ALICE. We can fill in some of the gaps later. Top of the stairs, second on the left. That's my room, use anything you want.

PEGGY. Thank you.

(PEGGY exits. ALICE stands at door for a moment then shouts.)

ALICE. Ned, are you still here?

(ALICE goes to pour herself a large drink. NED enters and quickly closes the door behind him.)

NED. What do you mean, 'Am I still here?' Consider it a holy miracle that I wasn't listening at the keyhole. Well? Tell all.

ALICE. Where's Panama?

NED. In the kitchen mending the toaster than he's going to make us all Eggs Benedict for lunch. That boy is the original tart with a heart of gold. A perfect treasure. I think you should seriously consider offering him a permanent contract.

ALICE. I don't wish to complicate my life any more at present, thank you.

(ALICE drains her glass.)

NED. My dear, should you be hitting the booze quite so strongly?

ALICE. Having unexpectedly become a mother twice in one day, I think I'm entitled to get totally paralytic.

NED. The cut and thrust of a caesarean, was it? How is the relationship with your daughter progressing?

ALICE. Ned please, I no longer trust myself to know anything. Your old friend is in severely extended shock vaguely waiting for all her hair and teeth to fall out.

NED. But you're not about to slash your wrists?

ALICE. Not before lunch, no.

NED. Good. I take it you are certain that this one is yours?

ALICE. Yes, not the faintest doubts. I have a daughter and the Cat's Home will probably have to be partially disinherited.

NED. Ah! In that case I have a question for you.

ALICE. Ned, stop interrogating me. Let me get things straight in my own mind first, alright?

NED. What I'm dying to ask is very basic. Just one little question.

ALICE. What?

NED. Who... is the father?

ALICE. Hogan... who else? Now leave well alone.

NED. I can't. Hogan was sterile. That was why those paternity suits never came to court.

ALICE. How in God's name did you find that out?

NED. Accidentally.

ALICE. He was rather ashamed of the fact, used to tell all the girls that he'd had a vasectomy. How accidentally do you mean?

NED. Pure chance. I just happened upon the medical report one day when I was looking for something to read. Gave me a nasty turn, I remember. Dead sperm—such a chilly contradiction.

(ALICE comes at him, gets a powerful grip on his arm and pulls him into the room away from the door.)

ALICE. Have you ever told anyone else?

NED. No, I thought it lacked interest.

ALICE. Peggy must never find out, it would be the end for her. She idolizes Hogan and she has more than enough to cope with in accepting me as her mother. Do you understand!

NED. I won't tell a soul. You have my solemn promise.

ALICE. It's very important.

NED. I'm convinced and so is my arm. Will you please release the tourniquet?

(ALICE lets go of him. NED rubs his arm.)

ALICE. I wonder if I'll get to like her eventually?

NED. Would you know where to begin?

ALICE. She's been under great stress. Mind you, she does seem to have an alarming temperament. She veers between love and hate like a weathervane in a hurricane. Quite capable of murdering me if she were to find out the truth.

NED. So quick, tell me who the father is.

ALICE. Why should I?

NED. Because confession is good for the soul and yours has taken a battering today. You might as well, you know you'll let it slip eventually.

ALICE. It could be one of two.

NED. I loathe riddles and puzzles. If you give me two sets of initials, I swear I shall strike you.

ALICE. You seem determined to shame me. I can't, it was over thirty years ago and my memory for casual names is not elephantine.

NED. A brief description will do.

ALICE. The most likely contender is a gentle tree surgeon who came to prune the ash tree.

NED. Yes, I can see that that might fail to thrill your darling daughter. And who's the outsider? One of the Royals?

ALICE. No, someone much closer to home.

NED. Anyone I know?

ALICE. Yes Ned, you know him well.

NED. So tell me.

(ALICE begins to tease him.)

ALICE. Are you quite certain you want to know? He's a very old friend.

NED. Yes, of course I do.

(ALICE gives him a wide smile and stares directly at him.)

ALICE. Sure? Very, very, very sure?

(NED catches on and begins to back away.)

NED. Oh no... no, that's impossible. Ridiculous. Insane!

ALICE. Dig out your old diaries, everybody else has, and check the date. You must have noted such a rare occurrence.

NED. You are being deliberately evil and vindictive, Alice
Hogan.

ALICE. We'll never know for sure but believe me, Ned
Jones is in there with a real chance.

(NED collapses in chair.)

NED. I could never have such a daughter.

ALICE. Oh, I don't know, I think she has your eyes. *(NED
glares at her.)* Yes, that's it. That vicious glare.

*(JOSEPH opens door in butcher's apron with cloth in his
hand.)*

JOE. Hurry, hurry, folks. Lunch is about to be served and
it's delicious.

ALICE. Thank you, Panama. We're on our way.

*(JOSEPH smiles and goes. ALICE extends hand to NED who
is sitting back with his eyes closed.)*

ALICE. Aren't you hungry, Daddy dearest?

(NED opens his eyes and takes her hand.)

NED. Promise me, you will never tell her.

ALICE. My lips are sealed.

*(ALICE pulls NED up out of chair and they half turned to exit
as PEGGY, well groomed again, appears in the doorway.)*

PEGGY. Hello.
NED. Oh, Peggy. Just for a second there you looked the image of your father, Hogan.

(NED exits past PEGGY.)

PEGGY. I think maybe I should get back to my hotel.
ALICE. Don't be silly, I don't want to lose you again. Stay to lunch.

(ALICE places her arm round PEGGY's shoulders and they begin to exit as curtain falls.)

END OF PLAY

PROPERTY LIST

<u>ACT I, Sc. 1</u>
Telephone
Black Hat (Alice)
Silver framed photo of Hogan
Business Card (Peggy)
Desk Diary
Large attache case with two books and papers inside
Camera and strap (Joe)
Canvas camera bag
Tray with coffee cup and glass of orange juice
small line drawing in passe partout surround

<u>Sc. 2</u>
Flower vase with some water.
Perfume atomizer
Small bunch of flowers wrapped in paper

<u>ACT II, Sc. 1</u>
Mug of coffee
Glass of orange juice
Plain jar with ashes in cardboard carton and wrapped in
        plain paper
Posy of flowers
Purse (Peggy)
With check book
Pill box
Notebook
Handkerchief (Ned)
Small leather case with
Bottle of colored sleeping capsules.

ABOUT ALICE
                      COSTUME PLOT

ACT I, Sc. 1
    ALICE: 1. Elegant black dress and hat
             2. A pretty summer dress
    NED: Grey suit, light shirt, black tie
    PEGGY: Pale blouse, smart, severe dark skirt and jacket
    JOE: Casual light colored summer suit, polo shirt

Sc. 2
    ALICE: A simple but expensive designer dress
    JOE: Pale chinos, dark jacket, blue shirt, dark tie

ACT II, Sc. 1
    ALICE: 1. White towelling robe, slippers
             2. Jeans and loose top
    JOE: 1. White towelling robe, barefoot
          2. Chinos, shirt, carrying jacket
    NED: Dark trouser, sports shirt
    PEGGY: Light colored shift dress

Sc. 2
    PEGGY: Light shift dress
    ALICE: Jeans and top
    NED: Trousers and sports shirt
    JOE: Chinos, shirt, butcher's apron

"ABOUT ALICE"

PATIO

SLIDING DOORS

FIREPLACE

WALL UNIT

chair

SOFA

STAIRS

TABLE

chair

DAYBED

DESK

WINDOW

Also By
Charles Laurence

About Alice

My Fat Friend

The Ring Sisters

Snap!

Please visit our website **samuelfrench.com** for complete
descriptions and licensing information

OTHER TITLES AVAILABLE FROM SAMUEL FRENCH

THE RING SISTERS
Charles Laurence

Farce / 4m, 3f / Interior

Silva Ring is a world famous singer with a severe hang up about her age. When a Swedish interviewer produces her true birth certificate, she resorts to increasingly desperate measures to prove him wrong. With help from her long term housekeeper Dolores, Silva pretends to be her own sister Iris, a tough lady who can make tough decisions. Silva's lover, a footballer, her agent and Dolores all suffer from the iron rule of Iris. Lola Wales, an old singer, is brought in to be an aunt and a petty forger is persuaded to attempt to destroy Silva's files at the Family Record Center. After a wild climax during which Silva scores a goal at Wembley Stadium, she can no longer juggle all her lies and subterfuges and escapes by having a bogus nervous breakdown. A victim of fame and wealth, she wins in the end and emerges stronger than ever.

OTHER TITLES AVAILABLE FROM SAMUEL FRENCH

GLENGARRY GLEN ROSS
David Mamet

Comedic Drama / 7m / 2 Interiors
This scalding comedy took Broadway and London by storm
and won the 1984 Pulitzer Prize. Here is Mamet at his very best,
writing about small-time, cutthroat real estate salesmen trying to
grind out a living by pushing plots of land on reluctant buyers in
a never-ending scramble for their share of the American dream.
Revived on Broadway in 2006 this masterpiece of American
drama became a celebrated film which starred Al Pacino, Jack
Lemmon, Alec Baldwin and Alan Arkin.

"Crackling tension... ferocious comedy and drama."
— *New York Times*

"Wonderfully funny... A play to see, remember and cherish."
— *New York Post*

MUSIC FROM DOWN THE HILL
John Ford Noonan

Drama / 2f / Interior

The setting is a psychiatric clinic atop a hill in the beautiful country town of Woodstock, New York. Claire Granick, a young schizophrenic who loves Bruce Springsteen to death and cannot for the life of her tell the truth, regularly drives out new roommates with terror tactics and Springsteen songs played too loud. Enter Margot Yossarian, a middle aged hysteric with a huge heart and a frightened body who also loves rock n roll, especially the music of the 60s: Hendrix, Joplin, The Doors, Cream. Claire's usually effective tactics don't undermine Margot, but rather release her stiffened body and send her to a soaring state of health dreamed of but never expected by the head of the hospital. In Act II, Margot attempts to help Claire break through her problems. Is she successful? Is rock n roll truly deep and loud enough to heal the mentally disturbed? Can the concept of rock penetrate the disturbed heart and create a miracle of mental health? Do people this disturbed ever successfully get back to the outside?

"A delicacy of feeling that is rare in theatre pieces today.... A cannily constructed melange of alienation [and] nostalgia..."
– *The New York Times*

SAMUELFRENCH.COM

www.ingramcontent.com/pod-product-compliance
Lightning Source LLC
Chambersburg PA
CBHW070638120726
47909CB00004B/1489